MW00978934

# Oh, Monkey

To Brennon
Enjoy!
Love Maryann
Burrows

Written &
Illustrated
by
MARY ANN
BURROWS

◆ FriesenPress

Suite 300 - 990 Fort St
Victoria, BC, V8V 3K2
Canada

www.friesenpress.com

**Copyright © 2019 by Mary Ann Burrows**
**Delta, British Columbia Canada**

First Edition — 2019

Illustrations in this book are from and under copyright of Burrowing Artist Studio.
Author photo by Sean Hitrec.

www.ohmonkey.net
ohmonkey@ohmonkey.net

All rights reserved.

No part of this publication may be reproduced in any form, or by any means, electronic or mechanical, including photocopying, recording, or any information browsing, storage, or retrieval system, without permission in writing from FriesenPress.

ISBN
978-1-5255-5901-3 (Hardcover)
978-1-5255-5902-0 (Paperback)
978-1-5255-5903-7 (eBook)

*1. YOUNG ADULT FICTION, GIRLS & WOMEN*

Distributed to the trade by The Ingram Book Company

Written & Illustrated by

MARY ANN BURROWS

Dedicated to my
ten-year-old self, and to
my Monkey.

Monkey chatters in my ear
all day long.

She tells me,
"You do nothing right!"

She tells me,
"You are wrong!"

# Oh, Monkey!

She's **been** with me throughout **my life,**

watches over me like a **star,**

# Oh,
# Monkey!

Whenever I do something **new**,
her **voice** begins to **quaver**.

She tries to make me **fearful**, and my **confidence** to **waver**.

We sat and had a **little chat**, my **Monkey** friend and **me**

I told her that I know she cares but need to set her free.

But she gets in **my mind** at times, and **won't** just let me **be.**

So, we agreed,
as good friends do, that she
could come along.

If she **sat still** and only said **kind words** that made me **strong**.

LIKE...

"You are **brave**,
and you are **kind**."

"I have your back.
High-five, my friend!"

I have to **say** we're doing **well**, since our little **chat**.

She sits there **now,**
says **nothing** much

...just smiles, and
tips her **hat.**

# Oh,
# Monkey!

And by the way I learned **today,**

my friend
Sean has one
too!

# More About
# Oh, Monkey!

Oh, Monkey! is an introduction to the concept of our inner critic and the idea
of seeing it as an entity separate from ourselves and one that we give life to. Being mindful of our disempowering thoughts can help us keep them at bay so that we can get on with enjoying the positive things in life.

Having an inner critic doesn't mean you are broken or need to be fixed, it's part of being human. Our self-esteem and self-image are formed by our thoughts and how we talk to ourselves. We all have two voices inside of us: one that is nurturing, and one that is critical. One voice lifts us up, and the other weighs us down. In an attempt to protect us from being hurt or disappointed, our inner critic tells us we aren't "enough." It's part of our ego system and it attacks our self-worth, telling us we aren't good enough, or smart enough, and stopping us from trying new things and being all we can be. We can learn to **turn off** the negative self-talk and take away its influence over us. We can learn to nurture ourselves by replacing it with the supportive, positive, and reassuring voice.

**Your critic is not you!** See if you can spot it when it comes around talking nonsense. Learn to talk back to your critic. You will soon see that the power is yours whether to argue with it, laugh at it, or ignore it. To learn to recognize and acknowledge it, it is fun to draw it and give it a name. What does your inner critic look like? Make it look as silly or scary as you want. .

I would love to see a picture of your inner critic! When you've drawn it, you can email it to me at ohmonkey@ohmonkey.net.

Wishing you wholesome peace of mind,
Mary Ann

# My Inner critic's name is

_____

# Tips for Disarming
# **Your Inner Critic**

The next time your inner critic chatters in your ear, first of all, embrace yourself with compassion. Thank it for its concern and create a new story.

Tell it:

I am.

I am open.

I am happy.

I am lovable.

I can do this.

I am grateful.

I learn as I grow.

I dare to be different.

I grow as I try new things.

I'm proud of my new skills.

I believe in myself and my abilities.

I deserve the better things life has to offer.

Thank you for loving me but I've got this one.

I appreciate you working so hard to keep me in line, but I am okay.

# About
# the Author

Mary Ann Burrows is the author and illustrator of

## Oh, Monkey!

She was born and raised in the Fraser Valley of British Columbia.

She is an artist a life and creativity coach.

Over the years she has enjoyed working with people to disarm their inner critics. This 'letting go' helps creativity to flourish, opening people up to new possibilities for joy through the expression of their own creativity.

She lives on a 72-acre farm near the ocean in Delta BC, and part time in Maui, Hawaii, with her family and her two dogs Pico and Theo.

Oh, Monkey! is an introduction to the concept of our inner critic.

We all have a 'Monkey.' It is the protective voice inside of us that tells us that we aren't "enough." To protect us from getting hurt, it will often say anything to keep us from trying new things. Listening to our Monkey affects our choices and self- confidence, causing us to second guess the things in life that our heart and soul desires.

This book is the ideal self-empowerment tool for young adults, offering insight and ideas on how to train a critical monkey with love and understanding.

Recommended for ages 10–12 and beyond.

CPSIA information can be obtained
at www.ICGtesting.com
Printed in the USA
LVHW071041131119
637156LV00003B/10/P